AF420321

Muppet Chainsaw Massacre

2

Bridget Chase

Copyright © 2017 Bridget Chase

The right of Bridget Chase to be identified as the Author of the Work has been asserted by him in accordance with the Copyright, Designs and Patents Act 1988.

First Published in 2017
By **Chase Entertainment**

All rights reserved. No part of this publication may be reproduced, stored in a retrieval system, or transmitted, in any form or by any means without the prior written permission of the publisher, nor be circulated in any form or binding or cover other than that in which it is published and without a similar condition being imposed on the subsequent purchaser.
All characters in this publication are fictitious and any resemblance to real persons, living or dead is purely coincidental.

BRIDGET CHASE
Muppet
Chainsaw
Massacre
2

Chapter 1

He gasped and sat up. Sweat beaded on his blue forehead. *Holy Fuck*!

It was the middle of the night and Grover sat panting in bed.

"Honey," Sarah rolled over, "Did you have another nightmare?"

Grover rubbed his head. "Yeah."

"About what happened?"

"Yeah," he said and tried to slow his racing heart. "I saw them all die again."

Sarah sat up. She wore an oversized white t-shirt. "Was Angel involved again?"

Grover nodded.

"And spike? Did you dream about him again too?"

He nodded. Grover got up. He wore white polka dot boxers. *Damn, I might never sleep an entire night ever again.*

Sarah clicked on a bedside lamp. "I don't know why you always bring Angel and Spike into your nightmare. They weren't even there and you know I love you, not them."

Grover poured a shot of whiskey. It was becoming a normal night routine. "Shee-it, it's not the Angel part keeping me up. Well you know what happened, you were there."

Sarah's head hung. She did know. She could see the bodies of her Muppet friends being torn apart. "You really need to consider getting some help. You are suffering."

He kicked back the liquid. It burned his throat. *Never strong enough to make me forget. Shit, how could you ever forget all your friends dying in front of your eyes by a chainsaw.* It had only been four months ago.

Grover climbed back under the covers.

Sarah rubbed his blue hairy chest. She could feel his frail ribs. *He's been losing more and more weight.* Sarah was worried.

Grover stared at the ceiling. The sound of the chainsaw ripping through stuffing filled the room. Sarah appeared over him. Her lips pressed against his.

"Not right now baby," Grover said, knowing he wouldn't get an erection.

Sarah rolled off him. "Okay, I was just hoping…"

"I know," he said, "Just turn the lamp off please."

Click!

Grover swallowed the fear in his throat. *I survived. I'm fine. I'm alive. But…* his mind fucked with him, *Leatherface was never caught.*

∞

Light traffic was on the street as Leatherface pumped gas into his VW bug. It had been an endless road trip.

With the tank filled he went inside to pay. Grabbing a Slim Jim off the counter he peeled the plastic back and started eating that shit.

"That'll be $21.95," The gas station worker said.

Leatherface dropped a few bills and left. He fought the urge to eat the face of the gas station worker. Something about it, maybe the texture, made him believe it would taste like a Lays potato chip.

He pulled out and got back on the highway. *Almost fucking there.* It was hard as fuck to track down the location. Luckily he was guided by evil itself. If there is one thing evil was best at, it was fucking finding its intended victim.

The check engine light came on. *Fuck*, that shit doesn't matter. Leatherface would drive until the car fucking died and then he would continue his journey by whatever means necessary.

He clicked the radio on. Mostly fucking static and nothing, out here in nowhere America. Then he found a station. Cindi Lauper's 'Time After Time' was playing.

It was the perfect song to continue his journey to Sesame street.

Chapter 2

"I'll see you later honey," Sarah said. She readied her purse at the door.

Grover leaned out the bathroom door, "Okay see you tonight."

"Oh, you are wearing the bowtie I like," she said.

He smiled.

"Bye," Sarah left.

Grover looked at the clock. Thirty minutes until he had to be at work.

Fuck, this is one of the biggest draw backs to leaving sesame street. *Stupid job.*

Grover had trouble finding work in L.A. Luckily, he found a gig working at a photography studio. He helped make the upset kids laugh.

Anyways, Grover put some eye drops in. *Wonder when I will ever start sleeping better*. Even leaving sesame street didn't help.

I guess seeing all your friends murdered and hacked apart like pigs, isn't something you get over easily.

He went to the kitchen and grabbed his bag lunch that Sarah made.

'Love you Honey' was written on a pink piece of paper inside along with his peanut butter and jelly sandwich, juice box, and animal crackers.

How did I ever get so lucky?

∞

Ms. Partea tried to focus her attention out the bus window. *My God! Just don't look at him.* She watched the trees and tried to not think about it. *How can I not think about it? Okay, maybe I should just move seats. What if he gets offended?*

Ms. Partea sat quietly. *Damn, he smells like…* Her stomach turned when she tried to name it. The scariest part about the person sitting next to her on the bus was the man's chainsaw.

Why would anyone bring a chainsaw on a bus?

The man began to eat. *Don't look, don't look, don't…* She glanced over.

The disfigured man of rot and curled flesh, bit into a strawberry filled donut. The thick red jelly inside popped out and dribbled down his chest.

Ms. Patrea gasped and looked away when he looked over.

He has no eyes. Just black pits. Oh lord, make this bus trip go by fast.

∞

"For our next breaking news story, we go live with corresponded Katy Slinger to tell us more about this Sesame Street murder," The news anchor said. "Ms. Slinger, what can you tell us about the horrible events that took place this morning?"

"Thanks for having me Bill," the TV screen cut to Katy Slinger standing in front of the recognizable Sesame Street sign. She wore a tight fitting white dress that showed off her tits, and she thought also made her ass look fabulous. Police and yellow tape framed the scene behind her.

"This morning Sesame Street became a street of nightmares when a crazed man armed with a chainsaw wreaked havoc. Now, the scene is too grizzly to show, but we have security cam footage from the bus. It appears when the bus arrived, the man killed fourteen people before heading to Sesame Street where he continued his massacre."

The TV showed black and white security footage.

Grover's mouth fell open and the bite of peanut butter sandwich fell onto the table. The footage showed Leatherface exiting the bus. Everything around him was blurred out. Grover knew why.

Katy came back on screen. "It is a real tragedy. Only four months ago, more than half the tenants of Sesame Street were murdered in Texas. The killer was never caught. It is being theorized that this might be the same killer, coming back to finish the job."

Grover felt sick to his stomach sitting in the claustrophobic break room.

"Police are actively searching for this suspect and advise that if anyone sees him, to lock themselves in their house and call the police. This man is armed and very dangerous."

Grover's eyes welled up. *Damn, everyone I ever loved is dead.* Then a new realization hit him.

Leatherface is taking a bus across the country? Shit! I'm fucking next!

Grover's guts felt watery. Sarah and he lived only forty-five minutes from Sesame Street.

∞

"Did you see the news?" Sarah asked when she entered their motel.

Bags were packed and Grover was folding some pants. "Yeah I did and we need to get the fuck away from here. Like, leave the fucking country or something."

"So you think he is coming for you?"

"Well yeah, don't you?"

Sarah put her purse down and came over to Grover. She wrapped her arms around him.

"Yes, I agree. Maybe the police will catch him."

Grover broke from the hug and threw the pants into a messy suitcase. "Hopefully they will catch him, but in the meantime, we need to go."

"Okay, let me pack my stuff," she went to the bathroom. Shouting, she called back to Grover, "So where do you think we should go?"

"Not sure," he zipped up the suitcase. *Almost finished. Not too bad.* "I've been thinking all day. I guess anywhere we have to fly and isn't accessible by car. I mean if he tried to fly…"

KNOCK, KNOCK, KNOCK!

Grover looked at the door.

Sarah peered out of the bathroom.

"Were you expecting anyone?" Grover asked.

"No."

KNOCK, KNOCK, KNOCK!

Grover's heart hammered. He looked at Sarah. Her face expressed the same thing as his, fear.

Chapter 3

Grover peered through the eye hole. *No one is there.* He looked back to Sarah and shook his head.

She made a funny confused face. The tension was so high Grover didn't even notice the fact that Sarah only wore small red shorts and a sexy black bra.

He decided to look out the peephole one more time.

BRRRR-RRRRRRRR-RRRRR!

Grover fell against the adjacent wall. *SHIT*!

Something ripped through the wall by the door.

A FUCKIN CHAINSAW! Grover froze.

Sarah screamed.

The scream pulled Grover out of his daze. He ran to Sarah. "Come on!" He grabbed her hand and headed to the window.

Shit, shit, shit!

He opened that fucker and Sarah climbed out. She exited to a back alley. *Good thing our motel room is on the ground floor*, she thought. The rough terrain abused her soft sexy feet.

Grover leapt out the window and hit a small privacy wall behind the motel.

Leatherface burst through the wall inside.

BRRRRRRR!

His chainsaw was raised overhead. He looked around.

Grover took one glance and ran through the dark back alley.

"Oh my God! He found us!" Sarah said. She panted as she pumped her arms. Her cupcake tits leapt cupped in the thin bra.

"Shit, if we make it to the car, we'll be okay!" Grover then realized. "OH FUCK!" he stopped.

"What?" Sarah asked.

BRRRRRRR!

They looked back.

Leatherface climbed stiffly out the window.

"I don't have the keys," Grover said.

They began to run.

BZZZZZ, BZZZZZZ!

Leatherface dragged his chainsaw along the brick siding.

Spark fucking flew and lit the night around him.

Sarah dared a look back and almost shit herself.

A fucking sparking nightmare in twisted skin and dark ill-fitting clothes raced in the black alley.

They came sprinting around the front of the motel.

"Wait by the car, I'll get the keys," Grover said.

"Okay."

They broke apart.

Grover laid on the speed. A cry built in his throat. He didn't have the fucking motel key but, *I can go through the hole that fuck cut*.

Sarah crouched and hid next to the car. She peered around the side.

BRRRRRRRRR!

Leatherface came through the parking lot. Smoke billowed from his chainsaw.

Looks like he is slowing down, Sarah thought.

Leatherface was about six doors away when Grover came flying out of the hole in the wall.

Shit, shit, shit!

"What is all this noise?" A door opened and a man in boxers, high socks, and wife beater came out.

The man didn't even manage to say, 'Oh shit,' before Leatherface's chainsaw let loose the man's guts onto the ground.

The man gurgled and Leatherface squealed like a pig at a breakfast buffet.

"Sarah?" Grover called out. *Oh thank god*!

She stood up by the passenger door.

Shit, shit, shit! Grover fumbled with the keys on the car door.

Click!

They both got in.

Damn! Grover started the car. Leatherface was almost on top of them.

The car came to life and he threw it into drive. Sarah screamed.

BRRRRRRRR! Leatherface cut the entire passenger side of the car with the chainsaw.

PSSSHHH, RRRRRRR, PSSSSHHHHH!

The car's tires were slashed and Grover lost control.

SMASH!

Airbags exploded in their faces.

"Oh God! Get out, hurry," Grover shouted.

Sarah pushed away the airbags. The roaring of a chainsaw was growing closer.

Grover opened the door.

RRREEEEEEE!

Sparks flew as the chainsaw contacted the metal frame.

Grover scrambled to the passenger seat and out Sarah's door.

They ran across the parking lot.

Leatherface squealed some Texas tune of death and hurried after them.

Cars honked and some men shouted things at Sarah as they

crossed the street. She was nearly nude. Her bare feet were hurting.

"Where do we go?" She asked.

Grover, with labored breaths said, "Fuck I don't know."

They raced down the sidewalk. Grover knew they couldn't just run forever.

Chainsaw teeth eating metal, erupted behind them. Shouts and screams sounded.

Leatherface lifted a person off the ground with his chainsaw. The teeth sheared them in half. Dark matter spilled on the ground and his weapon found another victim.

People fled their cars, metal crunched from accidents, and cries of agony filled the air, as Leatherface did his ballet of torture.

A police car sped down the street.

Grover and Sarah stopped to look back at the action.

Two more police cars came from the side streets.

This is it! Grover watched and felt like this was almost over.

"Police, put down your weapon!"

Leatherface lifted his chainsaw and squealed a Texas song with twang.

BRRRRRRR! The chainsaw played in the night air. The song was interrupted by gunfire.

Chapter 4

"Mmm…" Sarah slid her hand down Grover's stomach.

He tasted her sweet lips.

She wrapped her fingers around his hairy monster.

"Uhh." Grover cupped her tit.

"It's so good to be back," Sarah said.

"Yeah, it is. Never thought I would be able to come back to Sesame Street."

Grover was happy to be back. They had found a few other tenants. Nightly, Sarah and Grover have been working to repopulate Sesame Street. (Wink)

With the police killing Leatherface, Grover's nightmares stopped. The closure let him move on and now it was nothing but blue skies ahead.

∞

"Is he chipped?" Riley Finn asked the government doctor.

"Yes, the implant is in."

"And is it taking?"

"Take a look for yourself." The doctor pulled up the security camera feed in Leatherface's room. He picked up a microphone and said, "Riley is here, show him."

Riley watched the screen. A compartment in Leatherface's room opened and Leatherface hurried over.

"What is that?" Riley asked.

The doctor said, "We gave him a small pink stuffed animal. Just watch."

Riley watched Leatherface pick up the stuffed toy.

Suddenly Leatherface's face peeled open and some huge hideous mouth opened. He stuffed the cuddly animal into his big mouth and ate.

"What the fuck?" Riley starred. "This wasn't what I expected."

The doctor turned from the screen. "It wasn't what we expected either. The chip isn't effective."

Riley furrowed his brow and crossed his muscular arms, "What is he?"

"Well," the doctor said, " He isn't a demon like we thought. He is, the best I can describe, mutating."

"Mutating?"

The doctor cleared his throat. "Yes, mutating. He seems to be infected by some kind of virus. It healed him after the police shot him, and now, well, now it is altering him physically."

"So what is the virus?" Riley asked.

The doctor handed him a manila folder.

Riley opened it. His eyes scanned the document. "What is Racoon City?"

BAM! POW! Like a punch in the face by Adam West! If you like punches in the face, drag your ass to Bridget's website to see more author shit. Visit or don't, I got more shit to do. Peace.

https://chasebridget.wordpress.com